BY SIMAN NUURALI

ART BY ANJAN SARKAR

PICTURE WINDOW BOOKS
a capstone imprint

For my baba, who was and always remains my desert star. — S. N.

Sadiq is published by Picture Window Books,
a Capstone imprint
1710 Roe Crest Drive
North Mankato, Minnesota 56003
www.mycapstone.com

Library of Congress Cataloging-in-Publication Data
Names: Nuurali, Siman, author. | Sarkar, Anjan, illustrator.
Title: Sadiq and the Desert Star / by Siman Nuurali ; illustrated by Anjan Sarkar.
Description: North Mankato, Minnesota : Picture Window Books, [2019] | Series: Sadiq | Summary: Sadiq's father is going on a business trip, but before he goes he tells Sadiq a story of the Desert Star, which fits in perfectly with Sadiq's third-grade class field trip to the planetarium, and inspires Sadiq to build a simple telescope to study the stars when his father returns.
Identifiers: LCCN 2018050219 | ISBN 9781515838784 (hardcover) | ISBN 9781515845652 (pbk.) | ISBN 9781515838821 (ebook pdf)
Subjects: LCSH: Fathers and sons—Juvenile fiction. | Muslim families—Juvenile fiction. | Children of immigrants—Juvenile fiction. | Africans—United States—Juvenile fiction. | School field trips—Juvenile fiction. | Planetariums—Juvenile fiction. | CYAC: Fathers and sons—Fiction. | Muslims—United States—Fiction. | Immigrants—Fiction. | Africans—United States—Fiction. | School field trips—Fiction. | Planetariums—Fiction.
Classification: LCC PZ7.1.N9 Sad 2019 | DDC [Fic]—dc23
LC record available at https://lccn.loc.gov/2018050219

Design by Brann Garvey
Design Element: Shutterstock/Irtsya

Printed and bound in China.
1671

TABLE OF CONTENTS

HI, I'M SADIQ! MY FAMILY AND I LIVE IN MINNESOTA, BUT MY PARENTS ARE FROM SOMALIA. SOMETIMES WE SPEAK SOMALI AT HOME.
I'D LIKE YOU TO MEET MY FAMILY AND LEARN SOME INTERESTING FACTS AND TERMS FROM OUR CULTURE.

Baba
Hooyo
Nuurali
Aliya
Rania
Amina

FACTS ABOUT SOMALIA

- Most Somali people belong to one of four major groups: the Darod, Isaaq, Hawiye, and Dir.
- Many Somalis are nomadic. That means they travel from place to place. They search for water, food, and land for their animals.
- Somalia is mostly desert. It doesn't rain often there.
- The camel is an important animal to Somali people. Camels can survive a long time without food or water.
- Around ninety-nine percent of all Somalis are Muslim.

SOMALI TERMS

awoowe (ah-WOH-weh)—grandfather

baba (BAH-baah)—a common word for father

haa (HA)—yes

hooyo (HOY-yoh)—mother

salaam (sa-LAHM)—a short form of Arabic greeting, used by many Muslims. It also means "peace."

sambuus (sahm-BOOS)—fried pastries that are filled with spicy ground beef, chicken, fish, or vegetables

wiilkeyga (wil-KAY-gaah)—my son

CHAPTER 1

THE DESERT STAR

Sadiq squirmed in his chair. Recess was in five minutes. It was the first warm day of spring. The rest of the class was finishing a journal activity. Sadiq couldn't wait to play soccer with his friends!

"I have something special to share," Sadiq's third-grade teacher, Ms. Battersby, said. "Next weekend is our school's Spring Festival!"

Excited whispers went around the room.

"The festival is open to all," Ms. Battersby went on. "It's a chance for our school's teams and clubs to raise money. If you have a club, you can sign up to have a table. In the past, clubs have sold baked goods or crafts. See me if you need help thinking of something!"

Sadiq frowned. He wasn't part of a club.

Ms. Battersby looked around the classroom. "Now, before recess, I have one more announcement," she said. "On Thursday we'll be going to an observatory for a field trip!"

Sadiq sat up straight. He put his pencil down. He loved field trips!

RULES!
WORK HARD
BE KIND
Who? What? When? Where? Why? How?
Homework
Choose a planet from our solar system. Research your chosen planet and present what you find as a poster or piece of writing.

"This week, we're beginning a unit on space. We'll learn all about planets and stars. At the observatory, we'll view them in the night sky."

Sadiq looked over at his friends Zaza and Manny and grinned. He loved space! In the summertime he liked to look at the stars with his baba.

"Our field trip will be in the evening," Ms. Battersby said. "We'll need an adult at home to sign a special permission slip."

The teacher had just finished passing out the papers when the bell rang.

Sadiq, Zaza, and Manny raced to get to the soccer field first.

* * *

That night, Sadiq was brushing his teeth. He suddenly remembered the permission slip.

Still brushing, Sadiq went to his bedroom and found the paper. He hurried to his parents' room.

Baba was in the middle of packing for a business trip.

"Baba, can you sign this?" Sadiq asked. "My class is going to an observatory on Thursday!"

"Are you learning about space in school?" Baba asked. He took the permission slip and signed the paper.

"***Haa,*** Baba," said Sadiq. "Today we learned about Saturn. Did you know it has sixty-two moons?"

"I would like to hear about it, ***wiilkeyga***," Baba said as he handed the form back to Sadiq. "But you should finish brushing your teeth first!"

Sadiq hurried back into the bathroom and finished brushing.

"Make sure they are brighter than the white sands of Berbera!" Baba said.

Baba had been born and raised in the city of Berbera, Somalia. Sadiq loved hearing stories from his dad's childhood.

After brushing, Sadiq went to the bedroom he shared with his older brother, Nuurali. Nuurali went to bed much later than Sadiq, which sometimes made Sadiq jealous. He put the form in his backpack. Then he hopped into bed just as Baba was coming into the room.

"How long will you be gone, Baba?" Sadiq asked.

"Just a few days, little one. Let me tell you a story about the stars," Baba said. He sat on Sadiq's bed and tucked him in. "Do you remember how bright they were in Berbera?"

Sadiq nodded. He loved visiting Berbera. But he had only been twice because it was so far away. "They were bright like the streetlights!" Sadiq said.

Baba laughed. "Brighter than even your T-shirt!" He poked Sadiq's shoulder. Then he said, "But there is one star that was brighter than the rest. It is a star your **awoowe** calls the desert star."

"What's the desert star?" Sadiq asked.

Baba said, "When I was a boy, your awoowe would travel in his camel caravan through the desert. He sold bales of cloth and bought goods for our family. Whenever my baba left, I was sad. But as long as I could see the desert star, I knew he'd return safely."

"Where is the desert star?" Sadiq asked. "Can you show it to me?"

Baba shook his head. "We can't see it in the city because of all the light here. It's part of a cluster of five stars. The stars are in the shape of an arrow. The desert star is the largest and brightest star. It is at the very tip of the arrow. Next time we're in Berbera we'll look for it," Baba said, smiling.

"I can't wait!" Sadiq said.

"Now, you need to get some sleep, and so do I," Baba said. "My plane leaves early in the morning. Sleep well, Sadiq."

Sadiq took off his glasses and closed his eyes. He counted shooting stars until he fell into a deep sleep.

CHAPTER 2

THE OBSERVATORY

On Thursday, Sadiq, Zaza, and Manny were very excited for their field trip. They ran onto the bus, all talking at once.

"I bet we'll see the planets orbiting the sun," Zaza said.

"I hope we see a spaceship rocketing across the sky," said Manny.

Sadiq chose a window seat near the front of the bus. He liked to watch the landscape zoom by.

Zaza sat next to Sadiq on the aisle seat. They joked with their friends and told stories. Still, the bus ride seemed to take forever.

Finally Sadiq spotted a big building shaped like a dome. In front of the building was a spaceship.

"Zaza, look!" Sadiq said. He pointed out the window as the bus came to a stop.

"Whoa! Do you think an astronaut flew that to the moon?" Zaza asked excitedly.

"Let's find out!" said Sadiq. He, Manny, and Zaza ran off the bus toward the entrance.

* * *

Inside the building, Ms. Battersby led the class into a theater. Sadiq felt like he was at the movies! There were big chairs that leaned back. The lights were turned down. But instead of a screen at the front of the room, the screen was on the dome-shaped ceiling!

"Hello!" a voice echoed out. Everyone went quiet. "Welcome to the planetarium!" A man walked to the center of the room. "My name is Diego. I am a researcher here. This presentation will show you what conditions are like on the planet Mars. How many of you knew that Mars's surface is made up of red dust?"

Sadiq eagerly raised his hand.

"You kids know your stuff! Today we'll learn about why it's red. And we will learn a lot more about Mars. After the presentation, we'll visit the observatory upstairs. From there, we can observe the planet Mars," Diego said.

"Mars is really far away. Do you think we will be able to see it?" whispered Zaza to Sadiq.

"The telescopes are really big. I think so!" replied Sadiq.

"For now, please look up at the ceiling," Diego said.

Music started, and a video of the night sky played across the domed ceiling.

* * *

After a while, the closing credits rolled onto the screen. Sadiq jumped up from his seat right away. He couldn't wait to see the stars!

"That was such a cool movie," said Manny. "I didn't expect Mars to look as red as it did."

"Yes," agreed Sadiq. "I guess I thought it would look a little like Earth."

The class followed Diego upstairs to the observatory.

"The sun has set. The sky is clear," Diego said, as they entered a big room. "We have perfect conditions for viewing the planet Mars!"

The observatory was an open room, filled with all kinds of equipment. There were telescopes, computers, and maps of the night sky. Sadiq looked around in wonder.

There were several exhibits around the room. One explained how telescopes worked. Another one described how you could become an astronomer. Yet another exhibit explained what observatories are used for.

Sadiq went to an exhibit. He was so busy looking at a map of constellations that he got distracted.

He missed the instructions from Diego!

Become a
little astronomer!
MAKE YOUR
OWN TELESCOPE

When he turned around, Zaza was taking a turn at the telescope. Several of Sadiq's classmates were lined up behind him.

"Please get in line if you'd like to see Mars, Sadiq!" Ms. Battersby called. "We only have fifteen minutes before we need to get back on the bus."

Sadiq hurried over. After a few minutes of waiting in line, he stepped up to the telescope. He was relieved that he would get a turn.

Diego adjusted the eyepiece so it was at Sadiq's height.

"Look through there," Diego said. He pointed to the eyehole. "Do you see a small, pinkish circle in the sky?"

"Yes!" Sadiq said. "I wish I could go there."

"We all may *live* there one day, buddy," Diego said.

Sadiq stepped away from the telescope. "Really?" he said. His eyes widened.

"Really," Diego said. "Scientists and astronomers are studying if it's possible for humans to live there."

Sadiq's jaw dropped. "Cool!"

After Sadiq's turn at the telescope, Diego wrapped up their visit.

"Thank you, Diego!" the children said. They headed to the parking lot, talking excitedly about the planets and stars they had seen.

They waited outside for the bus to pick them up. Sadiq and a few of his classmates talked about their field trip.

"I wonder if we can see Mars in the sky now," a girl named Avina said.

Avina stared up at the sky. Soon the others joined her.

Sadiq, Zaza, Manny, Avina, and a boy named Odin all searched the sky for the pinkish-orange planet.

They weren't able to see anything other than some light clouds and distant stars.

"Why can't we see Mars?" Odin asked Ms. Battersby.

"We live near a big city. Cities have lots of light, and the light pollutes the sky," Ms. Battersby said. "Think of all the streetlights, office buildings, stores, and homes. The light coming from them blocks out some of the natural light of the stars. In the city it's harder to see the stars in the night sky."

"Then how come we could see Mars before?" Manny asked.

Sadiq had read about this at the museum. "Telescopes help because they collect all the light. They make the object seem brighter," he said.

"That's right, Sadiq!" Ms. Battersby said. "If you had a telescope right now, you'd be able to see Mars just as well as we did in the observatory."

"I wish we could see it whenever we want," Zaza said.

There has to be a way, thought Sadiq. Suddenly an idea came to him. "We can all start a club—the Space Club," he said. "Then we can raise money at the Spring Festival to buy a telescope!"

"Great idea," said Avina. "Let's all think about what we can sell."

"I'm in," said Odin.

"Me too," said Zaza.

Manny grinned. "Space Club taking off in . . . three . . . two . . . one . . ."

"Blastoff!" they all shouted.

CHAPTER 3

THE GREAT PLAN

"Would you like to say hello to your baba, Sadiq?" Hooyo asked. She held out her cell phone.

"Yes, please!" Sadiq said, taking the phone. "***Salaam,*** Baba!" he shouted into it.

"Salaam," Baba said. "How are you?"

"We had our field trip to the observatory yesterday," Sadiq said. "Do you know why Mars is red?"

"No, Sadiq," said Baba.

"It's because it has rusty red dust on its surface," said Sadiq. "Now I want a telescope so I can see Mars and other planets and stars and—"

"Whoa, slow down." Baba laughed. "I can barely keep up!"

"Sorry," Sadiq said. "I miss you."

Baba had been gone for two days. Sadiq was so happy to hear his voice.

"I miss you too, Sadiq," Baba said. "Tell me more about the stars you saw."

"We saw lots of stars from the observatory. We even saw Mars! But when we tried to see them outside, we couldn't. Ms. Battersby said it was because of light pollution," Sadiq said.

"Is that why you want a telescope?"

"Yes, Baba," Sadiq said.

"Telescopes are very expensive, wiilkeyga," Baba said.

"But my friends and I started the Space Club. What if we raise a lot of money?" Sadiq asked.

"Ask your brother to help you do some research," Baba said. "You can see if you think it's possible."

After they hung up, Sadiq went to his room to ask Nuurali for help.

"Nuurali! Baba says you have to help me!" Sadiq called. He ran down the hallway toward his bedroom.

Nuurali was lying on his bed, reading a sports magazine. He let out a big sigh.

"I need your help looking up telescopes to buy," Sadiq said. He went over to Nuurali's desk and grabbed his brother's laptop.

"Okay, fine," Nuurali said. He sat up. "But only if you'll do my chores for today. You have to set the table for dinner and bring in the mail."

"Fine," Sadiq said. He gave the laptop to his brother and sat beside him on the bed.

Nuurali did a quick internet search.

Sadiq was shocked. Most telescopes cost hundreds of dollars.

"Maybe you can ask for one for a birthday gift instead, Sadiq," Nuurali said, shaking his head.

Sadiq sighed. His birthday wasn't for months. "We could probably make one on our own for much less. And it'd be a lot more fun!" he said.

"That's not a bad idea, Sadiq!" said Nuurali. "Let's see if we can find some instructions online."

Nuurali clicked around the website while Sadiq peered at the screen.

"It says here you would only need a few supplies," Nuurali said. He pulled up the list for Sadiq to read.

- paper towel tubes
- 2 convex lenses
- paint
- tape
- scissors

"It looks like you could get the supplies for about twenty dollars," Nuurali said.

"We could definitely raise that much money at the Spring Festival!" Sadiq said.

It was decided. The Space Club would build a telescope themselves!

CHAPTER 4

SAMBUUS

The next day, the five Space Club members all sat in a circle outside at recess.

"Welcome to the first meeting of the Space Club!" Sadiq said. "Over the weekend, I found out that telescopes can be very expensive. But I have an idea. We can build one instead."

"That sounds like fun!" Manny said.

"Nuurali and I found videos online that had directions," Sadiq said. "We can use the money we raise at the Spring Festival to buy the supplies."

"That's a great idea!" Odin said. "I love to build things."

"What's everyone going to sell at the Spring Festival?" Avina asked. "My mom and I can bake something. Her chocolate chip cookies are delicious."

"I'll see if my grandma can make lemonade," Manny said. "It's going to be hot out this weekend."

"I'll print out stickers with planets and stars on them," Odin said.

"And I can make some paintings of planets and constellations," Zaza said.

Sadiq was getting excited. "Now I just have to think of something!" he said.

* * *

That night, Sadiq was thinking of things to sell at the festival. A lovely smell drifted into his room. ***Sambuus!***

Sadiq loved sambuus, or samosas. But usually his mother only cooked them during Ramadan. It wasn't Ramadan.

Why would Hooyo be cooking sambuus tonight? Sadiq wondered.

Sadiq wandered into the kitchen. His mother and Aliya were chopping vegetables.

"Are we having sambuus for dinner?" Sadiq asked.

Aliya nodded. "I asked Hooyo to make them. She said she would if I helped."

That gave Sadiq an idea. "Hooyo, could you make sambuus for the Space Club to sell at the Spring Festival this weekend?" he asked.

"Okay, Sadiq, but I'll need your help. Sambuus are a lot of work," Hooyo said.

"I'll help!" Sadiq said.

* * *

The day before the Spring Festival, Sadiq, Aliya, and Hooyo went grocery shopping. Sadiq picked out his favorite fillings for sambuus—ground beef, bell peppers, cilantro, onions, and carrots.

When they got home, Sadiq and Aliya set up their cooking stations.

Aliya chopped up the fillings. Sadiq rolled out the dough. Hooyo added spices to the mixture. She cooked the sambuus on the stovetop.

When they were done, there were enough sambuus to feed the whole neighborhood. Sadiq couldn't wait to show his friends.

CHAPTER 5

THE SPRING FESTIVAL

Sadiq waved excitedly from the car. "Zaza!" he shouted as he got out. "Wait till you see what I brought."

It was the day of the Spring Festival, and Zaza was unloading supplies from his mother's car. He stopped what he was doing and rushed over to see.

In Hooyo's trunk there were many containers filled with sambuus.

"Sambuus! Yum!" Zaza said. "Can we have some?" He looked hopefully at Sadiq's mother.

"Zaza, manners!" his mother said, walking over from her car.

Hooyo laughed. "I think there will be enough to go around, Zaza. First let's get this table set up."

Zaza's and Sadiq's mothers each grabbed a side of the folding table and carried it inside the school. The boys followed, carrying the food items.

Inside, the rest of the Space Club was setting up. Avina arranged a plate of cookies. Odin and Manny put Manny's grandmother's lemonade on the table.

Children, parents, and neighbors had started coming. Soon the Space Club members were busy selling their items. They explained why they were raising money.

Everyone seemed very interested. They were especially excited when Sadiq told them that they would be able to see Mars through their telescope.

At the end of the day, they counted all the money. Forty-two dollars!

"Now we just need to buy these materials," Sadiq said. He held out a list to show his friends.

"I have paper towel tubes," Odin said. "We collect them for our gerbil to climb through."

"And I have paint," said Manny.

"I'll bring tape," said Avina.

"And I'll cover the scissors," said Zaza.

"That leaves the convex lenses to me," said Sadiq. "Forty-two dollars will definitely cover it."

"I'll place the order for you, Sadiq. You can pay me back," Hooyo said. "The package should arrive in a couple of days. Then you all can come over to put the telescope together."

"Next meeting is Tuesday after school at my house!" Sadiq said.

"Maybe we can even look at the stars once it gets dark out," Avina said.

The Space Club members all agreed.

"Three . . . two . . . one . . . blastoff!"

CHAPTER 6

THE STARGAZING PARTY

"HOOYO!" Sadiq shouted. He ran down the stairs to the kitchen. He was almost in tears. The convex lenses had arrived yesterday. Sadiq had put them in his closet. But now one of them was gone!

"Sadiq," Hooyo said. She hugged him. "Please calm down and explain what's the matter."

"One of my lenses is gone. I can't find it," Sadiq said, still sobbing.

“Maybe one of the twins took it. They might have thought it was a toy,” Hooyo said. She rubbed Sadiq’s back.

“I already checked their room!” Sadiq cried. “The Space Club meeting is in an hour. How am I going to explain it to them?”

“I might have an idea of where it is. . . .” Hooyo said. “Follow me.”

Hooyo led him into the girls' bedroom. A dollhouse sat in the corner of the room.

"Aha!" Hooyo said. She walked over to the dollhouse. She bent down and reached inside. "Is this your missing lens?"

"Yes!" Sadiq said. "How did you know it was there?"

"Amina's been taking things she shouldn't. She stores them in here. It must be a phase." Hooyo sighed. She handed the lens to Sadiq.

Just then, the doorbell rang. Sadiq raced downstairs to answer it. When he opened the door, Odin and Manny waved at him.

"Hi!" Sadiq said. "Are you ready to start building the telescope? Avina and Zaza should be here soon."

"Yes!" Odin and Manny said. They followed Sadiq into the living room.

Hooyo brought in some snacks for the Space Club. The group settled down to put together their telescope. Sadiq, Odin, and Manny dug into the food. They began to arrange the supplies.

Then the doorbell rang again. Sadiq's mother answered it. Minutes later, Avina and Zaza joined them in the living room.

"Let's get to work, Space Club!" Sadiq said.

* * *

The Space Club spent the afternoon building the telescope. They closely followed the instructions in the videos.

When they'd finished, there was still about an hour until the sun set.

"What if we invite some of my neighbors over? They might want to look through our telescope," Sadiq said.

"Good idea," said Avina.

"We could call it a stargazing party," said Odin.

Sadiq, Avina, Manny, Odin, and Zaza walked around the block. They invited neighbors to come look at the stars through their telescope once it got dark outside.

They headed back to Sadiq's house to start setting up. Outside his house, Sadiq spotted a familiar car.

"Baba!" Sadiq cried. He ran to hug his father, who was just getting out of the car.

"Hi, Sadiq!" Baba said. "Your mom told me there's a stargazing party going on."

"Yes, Baba. My club made a telescope," Sadiq said.

"Stellar work, Space Club!" Baba said.

Now the sun had almost set. It was time! Baba helped Sadiq and his friends set up the telescope on the deck.

Sadiq's neighbors, family, and friends were all gathered in the backyard for the party. They talked and laughed as they took turns at the telescope. Sadiq decided to tell everyone about the desert star.

"When my baba was young," Sadiq explained, "his dad—my awoowe—would go into the desert to sell cloth. My baba would miss him when he was gone. Awoowe showed him a bright star in the eastern sky. He called it the desert star. If Baba could see it every evening, it meant his father was safe. He would return home soon. But here, we're far from the desert. It's really hard to spot the desert star."

Baba smiled at Sadiq. "Wiilkeyga," he said, "how about we see if we can find that desert star with your new telescope?"

"Cool!" Sadiq said. He ran toward the stairs to the deck. "Wanna race, Baba?" he asked.

"Are you sure about that?" Baba asked, smiling.

"Three . . . two . . . one . . . blastoff!" Sadiq shouted, and he took off.

He and his father raced each other up the stairs to the deck. They were ready to explore space.

SPACE CLUB

GLOSSARY

astronaut (AS-truh-nawt)—someone who travels in a spacecraft

astronomer (uh-STRAH-nuh-mer)—someone who studies stars, planets, and space

caravan (KAIR-uh-van)—a group of people using animals or vehicles to travel together

condition (kuhn-DISH-uhn)—the general state of a person, animal, or thing

constellation (kahn-stuh-LAY-shuhn)—a group of stars that forms a shape and usually has a name

convex (kahn-VEKS)—curved outward, like the outside of a bowl

equipment (i-KWIP-muhnt)—the tools, machines, or products needed for a particular purpose

exhibit (ig-ZIB-it)—an object or collection of objects on display in a museum

observatory (uhb-ZUR-vuh-tor-ee)—a special building that has telescopes or other instruments for studying the stars

orbiting (OR-bit-ing)—traveling in a circular path around something

planetarium (plan-uh-TAIR-ee-uhm)—a building with equipment for copying the positions and movements of the sun, moon, planets, and stars by projecting their images onto a curved ceiling

Ramadan (RAH-muh-dahn)—the ninth month of the Muslim year, when Muslims fast each day from sunrise to sunset

researcher (REE-surch-er)—a person who collects information about a subject through reading or experimenting

stellar (STEL-ur)—relating to stars; also can mean outstanding

TALK ABOUT IT

1. Sadiq and his friends each contribute something to sell at the Spring Festival. What would you sell to raise money for the Space Club?

2. Sadiq likes the planet Saturn, because it has sixty-two moons. What is your favorite planet in the solar system? Explain what you like about it.

3. Nuurali helps Sadiq research telescopes on the computer. Think of something you have had to research online recently. What did you learn about it?

WRITE IT DOWN

1. Baba tells a story to Sadiq—the story of the desert star. Write a poem about the desert star, imagining that you're seeing it from Sadiq's awoowe's caravan.

2. Sadiq learns about his baba's childhood when he hears the story of the desert star. Interview someone in your family about their childhood. Where did they grow up? What did they like to do? Whom did they live with? Write a paragraph about what you learn.

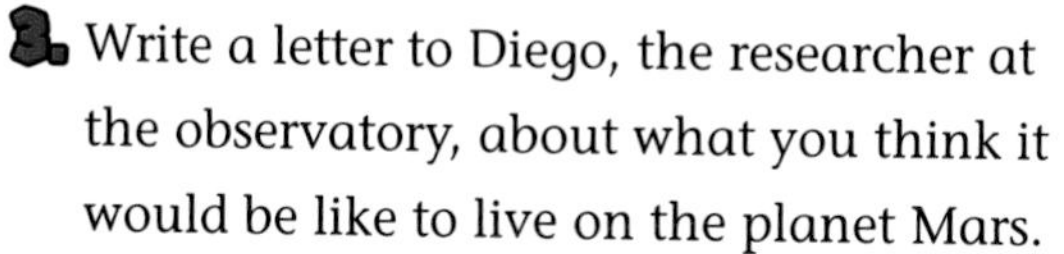

3. Write a letter to Diego, the researcher at the observatory, about what you think it would be like to live on the planet Mars.

TELESCOPE AT HOME!

Do you want to build a telescope like the one Sadiq and his friends made? With a few simple pieces, you can make your own telescope and view the moon and stars in the night sky!

WHAT YOU NEED:

- paper towel tubes
- 2 convex lenses (from old reading glasses or ordered online)
- scissors
- tape
- paint
- markers
- crayons

WHAT TO DO:

1. Take one of the paper towel tubes and use a pair of scissors to cut through it lengthwise until it is open. It should look like the letter *U* from the side. Close it so one side overlaps the other.

2. Put the tube you've cut into the other paper towel tube and let it expand so it fits tightly.

3. Place one of the lenses on the outside of the inner tube with the curved side facing into the tube. Tape it to make sure it stays in place.

4. Place the second lens on the outside of the outer tube with the curved side facing away from the tube. Tape this in place, making sure to not cover up too much of the lens with tape.

5. Using paint, markers, crayons, and whatever art supplies you'd like, decorate the tubes to make your telescope look cool!

6. At night, use the telescope to look at the stars and the moon! Make sure you don't use the telescope to look at the sun during the day.

CREATORS

Siman Nuurali grew up in Kenya. She now lives in Minnesota. Siman and her family are Somali—just like Sadiq and his family! She and her five children love to play badminton and board games together. Siman works at Children's Hospital, and in her free time, she also enjoys writing and reading.

Anjan Sarkar is a British illustrator based in Sheffield, England. Since he was little, Anjan has always loved drawing stuff. And now he gets to draw stuff all day for his job. Hooray! In addition to the Sadiq series, Anjan has been drawing mischievous kids, undercover aliens, and majestic tigers for other exciting children's book projects.